This book is dedicated to my family and friends for all their love and support. My daughter, specifically, has been my partner from day one in the brainstorming stage.

My son has been the "toddler tester" who has given genuine laughs and honest reactions to the story along the way.

Of course, I cannot leave out Chiara, who was able to bring the words to life with adorable and emotional illustrations. Without these people, this book would not be a reality. I will be forever grateful to the Mascot Books team for helping me share laughter and joy with young children, and for creating wonderful memories for me to share with my daughter and son during the entire publishing process.

www.mascotbooks.com

Baby Squashy Face

For more information, please contact:
Mascot Books
620 Herndon Parkway, Suite 320
Herndon, VA 20170
info@mascotbooks.com

Library of Congress Control Number: 2018903405

CPSIA Code: PRT0618A
ISBN-13: 978-1-68401-780-5

Printed in the United States

BABY SQUASHY FACE

Becky Carlyle

Illustrated by
Chiara Civati

*May you always feel loved,
even when things get messy!
9-8-18*

Becky Carlyle

Something is cooking,
but what can it be?
Whatever it is, it'll soon
be on me!

I'm in my highchair ready to eat.
Your spoon is coming in with
your yummy squashy treat.

What's this mushy stuff in my mouth?
I hear you telling me to chew,
but the squash runs down my chin.
My tongue doesn't know what to do!

Chewing doesn't seem to work that great.
I'll need to try something else at this rate.

Maybe I should spit and make squash drool! Uh oh! By the look on your face, spitting isn't cool.

How about I play with
the spoon?
I'll smear it on my cheeks
all afternoon.

I'll put the squash all through my hair.
It feels much better up in there.

Maybe I'll make squash boogies.
That'd be quite a sight.
I'm going to need a bath tonight.

This tickling in my nose makes me want to sneeze! ACHOO! Sorry Mommy! Now you're messy too.

Nothing seems to work! I just want to eat some of Mommy's tasty squash treat.

Instead, it's up my nose and between my toes. It's in my hair and all over my clothes!

"Oh baby! Your squashy
face is so sweet.
It almost looks good
enough to eat.

But the squash belongs
in your mouth, my dear,
not in your belly button,
armpit, or ear."

Just in my mouth you say?
I guess I can try it that way.

Mmmm! The squash tastes SO good!
I'm getting better at eating like I should.

There may be squash globs all over the place,
but that's okay—just look at my adorable face!

Making a mess isn't a big deal.
It's how I show love for my first squashy meal!

About the Author

Becky is a trained mezzo-soprano singer and holds a Bachelor of Music degree from Iowa State University. As a former K-12 vocal music teacher and youth symphony manager, Becky has spent her career enriching children educationally, creatively, and artistically. Becky has spent years writing grants, initially as part of her previous manager position, and continues to write on a case-by-case basis.

Now as a stay-at-home mom, Becky enjoys photography and writing children's picture books, but above all she is passionate about being a wife, mom, and friend. Experiencing life with children has given Becky a deeper perspective on what's most important in life. This book started as a fun summer project to spend special one-on-one time with her daughter (after all, Becky knows it's not always easy to share Mom with a little brother).

The mom-daughter duo has excitedly spent almost a year bringing *Baby Squashy Face* to life and hopes you have as many great laughs reading the book as they did making it.

About the Illustrator

Chiara Civati is a children's illustrator based out of Italy, where she lives and works in a small town on Como Lake.

After studying fashion and textile design in high school, Chiara went on to study visual design and illustration at her college in Milan. Chiara eagerly started her work illustrating books and writing stories for children right after graduation, and hasn't stopped since.

She has been known to illustrate and publish her own stories that she's written, but more often, she spends her time working as a freelance illustrator which is what she loves most. When she's not busy at work, she loves to read books, especially fairy tales, and loves to travel around the world so she can continue being inspired by everything the world has to offer.